Hello, Family Members,

Learning to read is one of the most important accomplishments of early childhood. **Hello Reader!** books are designed to help children become skilled readers who like to read. Beginning readers learn to read by remembering frequently used words like "the," "is," and "and"; by using phonics skills to decode new words; and by interpreting picture and text clues. These books provide both the stories children enjoy and the structure they need to read fluently and independently. Here are suggestions for helping your child *before*, *during*, and *after* reading:

Before

- Look at the cover and pictures and have your child predict what the story is about.
- Read the story to your child.
- Encourage your child to chime in with familiar words and phrases.
- Echo read with your child by reading a line first and having your child read it after you do.

During

- Have your child think about a word he or she does not recognize right away. Provide hints such as "Let's see if we know the sounds" and "Have we read other words like this one?"
- Encourage your child to use phonics skills to sound out new words.
- Provide the word for your child when more assistance is needed so that he or she does not struggle and the experience of reading with you is a positive one.
- Encourage your child to have fun by reading with a lot of expression . . . like an actor!

After

- Have your child keep lists of interesting and favorite words.
- Encourage your child to read the books over and over again. Have him or her read to brothers, sisters, grandparents, and even teddy bears. Repeated readings develop confidence in young readers.
- Talk about the stories. Ask and answer questions. Share ideas about the funniest and most interesting characters and events in the stories.

I do hope that you and your child enjoy this book.

—Francie Alexander
Reading Specialist,
Scholastic's Learning Ventures

For Virginia Bauer,
my warm and wonderful mother
—J.B.S.

ISBN 0-439-20546-8

Text copyright © 2000 by Judith Bauer Stamper.
Illustrations copyright © 2000 by Tim Raglin.
All rights reserved. Published by Scholastic Inc.
SCHOLASTIC, HELLO READER, CARTWHEEL BOOKS, and
associated logos are trademarks and/or registered trademarks of Scholastic Inc.

Library of Congress Cataloging-in-Publication Data
Stamper, Judith Bauer.
    Five haunted houses / by Judith Bauer Stamper ; illustrated by Tim Raglin.
        p.   cm. — (Hello reader! Level 4)
    "Cartwheel Books."
    Contents: Five brief spooky tales about some of the funny and not so funny
things that can happen in haunted houses.
    ISBN 0-439-20546-8 (pbk.)
    [1. Haunted houses — Fiction. 2. Ghosts—Fiction. 3. Halloween—Fiction.]
I. Raglin, Tim, ill. II. Title. III. Series.

PZ7.S78612Fj   2000
[E] — dc21   00-026572

10 9 8 7 6 5   04

Printed in the U.S.A.
First printing, October 2000

23

FIVE HAUNTED HOUSES

by Judith Bauer Stamper
Illustrated by Tim Raglin

Hello Reader! — Level 4

SCHOLASTIC INC.
New York   Toronto   London   Auckland   Sydney
Mexico City   New Delhi   Hong Kong

ARE YOU AFRAID OF GHOSTS?

High on a hill sat an old house.

Its windows were broken.

Its shutters creaked.

Bats flew in and out of the chimney.

Kids walked faster when they passed by it.

Everyone said it was a haunted house.

Everyone but Jake.

Jake didn't believe in ghosts.

One night, Jake and his friend

walked by the house.

His friend wanted to run.

Jake stopped right in front.

"Are you coming in with me?" he asked.

"Not me!" his friend said.

Then he took off running.

"Chicken!" Jake yelled after him.

Jake stood on the sidewalk all alone.
He looked up at the house.
A big full moon shone down on it.
Jake felt a shiver creep up his spine.

"I'm not afraid of ghosts!" Jake said
to himself.
Then he walked right up to the house.
He knocked on the door three times.
KNOCK! KNOCK! KNOCK!

The door swung right open.
Jake peeked inside. Nobody was there,
so he walked on in.

Jake went into the living room.
The only light was from the fireplace.
Everything looked dark and shadowy.

Jake went up to a big chair
in front of the fireplace.
He sat down.
Then he just about jumped out of his skin!

A girl was sitting in the chair
just across from him.
She smiled at Jake.
"What's wrong?" she asked.
"Are you afraid?"

"I'm not afraid of anything," he said.
"Me neither," said the girl.

"My friends are afraid of this house,"
Jake said. "But I'm not."
"Me neither," said the girl.

Jake frowned.
This girl had to be afraid
of something.
Maybe he could scare her.

"Everyone says this house is haunted,"
Jake said. "But I'm not afraid of ghosts."
"Me neither," said the girl.

Then she smiled at Jake.
And disappeared.

YOU'LL BE SORRY

Lisa was visiting her aunt and uncle.
They lived in an old house
filled with strange things.
Some people said the house was haunted.
But Lisa didn't care.
She liked scary stuff.

She liked the fireplace that threw
scary shadows on the wall.

She liked the tall windows that rattled
like bones in the wind.

She liked the winding staircase that had
old, creaky steps.

Most of all, she liked the marble statue
at the bottom of the staircase.

The statue was of an old man.
His marble face was set in an awful frown.
In his twisted hands he held a handkerchief.
The weirdest thing was, he wore a pair of
thick, wool socks over his marble feet.

Lisa wondered what was under
those wool socks.
"Can I take off his socks?" Lisa asked
her uncle.
"You'll be sorry if you do," her uncle said.
"So don't!"

Lisa passed the statue every time she went up and down the stairs.
She was dying to find out what was under those socks!

Lisa looked around. She reached out to touch the socks.
Just then, her aunt came by.
"Can I take off his socks?" Lisa asked her aunt.
"You'll be sorry if you do," her aunt said.
"So don't!"

That night, Lisa went up to her bedroom.
She pretended to go to sleep.
But instead, she waited until the house was
dark and quiet.
Then she crept down the stairs.

The statue waited for her at the bottom of
the steps.

It was lit by moonlight coming in from
a window.

Lisa looked at its frowning face.

She looked at its twisted hands.

Then she looked down at the socks.

Finally, she would find out what was
under them!

Her hands trembled as she reached out
for the socks.

Then, quickly, she pulled both socks off.

"EEEEEWWWWW!!!!" Lisa screamed.
Under the socks were two … horrible …

SMELLY FEET!

A TERRIBLE FRIGHT!

Five little ghosts
lived in a haunted house.

"EEEK!" said the first.
"I just saw a mouse!"

"Help!" said the second.
"There's a spider on the wall!"

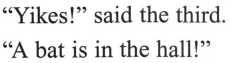

"Yikes!" said the third.
"A bat is in the hall!"

"Yuck!" said the fourth.
"There's a lizard on the floor."

"Uh-oh!" said the fifth.

"I hear a knocking on the door."

Then ... *Ooooooo* went the wind,
and out went the light.

And the five little ghosts
got a terrible fright!

RAP, RAP, RAP!

Luis couldn't believe his eyes.
His new house was a nightmare!
And his family was moving in
that very night.

Luis followed his mother and father
up to the house.
The front steps creaked and moaned.
His father opened the door.
It creaked and groaned.
They all walked inside.

Luis looked around.

The inside was just as bad as the outside.

Old. Dusty. Dark.

And creepy!

"I won't live here," Luis said to his mother and father.

They just smiled and patted his head.

"You'll get used to it, Luis," they said.

Luis climbed the stairs to his bedroom.
His footsteps echoed through the house.
He kept stopping to look around.
Was something following him?

Luis went straight into his room.

He jumped right into bed.

He turned off the light.

Then he pulled the sheet up over his head.

Everything was quiet... as quiet as a tomb.

Then Luis heard a sound.

It went...

RAP! RAP! RAP! TAP! TAP! TAP!

And something pulled the sheet off
Luis's bed!

"EEEEEEKKKKKK!!!!!!!"
Luis screamed his head off!

Luis's mother and father came running.

They put his sheet back on him.

They sang him songs.

They told him it was just a bad dream.

But Luis knew better!

The next night, Luis climbed the stairs to
his bedroom.
His footsteps echoed through the house.
He kept stopping to look around.
Was something following him?

Luis went straight into his room.
He jumped right into bed.
He turned off the light.
Then he pulled the sheet up over his head.

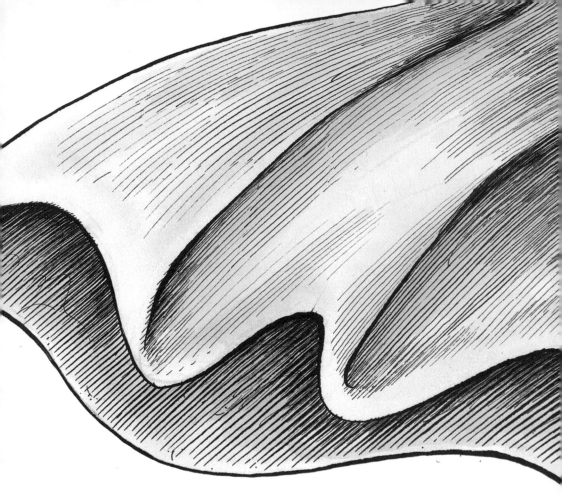

Everything was quiet... as quiet as a grave.
Then Luis heard a sound.
It went...
RAP! RAP! RAP! TAP! TAP! TAP!
And something pulled the sheet off
Luis's bed!

"EEEEEKKKKKKK!!!!"
Luis screamed his head off again.

Luis's mother and father came running.

"Luis, stop screaming!" they said.

"You've just had a bad dream."

"It wasn't a dream," Luis said.

"And I won't live here one more night!"

There was nothing his parents could do.

Luis would not stay in the house.

They had to pack up and move.

The next day, Luis carried all his things
down the staircase.

His footsteps echoed through
the empty house.

He kept stopping to look around.

Was something following him?

Luis put all his things in the trunk.
Then he got into the backseat of the car.
Luis watched the house as they drove away.
He never wanted to see that house again!

Everything was quiet in the car... as quiet as a coffin.

Then Luis heard a sound coming from the trunk.

It went...

RAP! RAP! RAP! TAP! TAP! TAP!

And a little voice whispered into Luis's ear...

"So, where are we going?"

THE GREEN DOOR

It was Halloween, the spookiest night of
the year!
Tom couldn't wait to go trick-or-treating.
This year, he was dressing up as a vampire.

Tom put fangs on his teeth.
He painted his face white.
He threw a black cape around his shoulders.
Then he got his bag for treats.

Tom went to meet his friend Ben.
Ben had just moved to an old house.
It sat on the edge of town.
Tom had not been there yet.
But he knew it had a green door.

Tom walked along the streets.
The night was very dark.
A full moon was in the sky.

Everyone was out trick-or-treating.
Monsters. Mummies. Vampires. Witches.
Tom felt a little afraid.
He couldn't wait to get to Ben's house.

He walked and walked to the edge of town.
All the houses were old and gloomy.
Then he saw it ... the house with the
green door.
He walked up and rang the doorbell.

A monster opened the door.
"Hi, Ben," Tom said.
A noise came out of the monster's mouth.
It sounded like, "GRUMF."
"Are you ready to go trick-or-treating?"
Tom asked.
"GRUMF!" the monster answered.
"I like your costume," Tom said.
"GRUMF!" the monster answered.

The two friends went from house to house.
"Trick-or-treat!" Tom said.
"GRUMF!" the monster answered.

Their treat bags got fuller and fuller.
"I love Halloween," Tom said.
"GRUMF!" the monster answered.

They went up to the next house.
It was old.
It had a green door.

Tom rang the doorbell.
"Trick-or-treat!" he yelled.
Ben opened the door.
"Where have you been?" Ben asked.

Tom's eyes got bigger and bigger.
He turned around.
"GRUMF!" answered the monster.

Then it ran off into the night.